BRING YOUR

MICCC

IMAGE

BRING YOUR MICCC

IMAGE

DIAMOND WILSON

In no way is the content in this book meant to provide counsel, either emotional, psychological, or financial, to the reader. The information contained in this book is opinion only, and is based on a unique perspective and experience. The author and contributors are not professional financial managers nor crisis counselors, and are not certified to give legal, psychological, or financial advice. All decisions that are made and acted upon by the readers regarding their well-being are their responsibility alone.

First LonnaDee Press paperback edition, 2018
Printed in the United States of America
ISBN: 978-0-9898594-4-8

Word-refining done by Mark Schultz at wordrefiner.com

Cover art by Vanessa Flores
Cover photo by Shawn O'Connell

Visit: diamondwilson.com

To Matthew. May the man in the mirror become the man of the mind.

CONTENTS

INTRODUCTION

The purpose of this book is not to be limiting, but rather to open up a world of possibilities and unique combinations that will allow you to truly stand apart from the crowd.

"Image" in this book is not to be confused with anything superficial. It's not about the brands you wear, the styles you choose, or the color of your hair, skin, or fingernails, or how many piercings you have. "Image" refers to the essence of your very being, the self that exists without any of those things—the self who looks out through your eyes, feels through your fingertips, and recognizes scents, sounds, and tastes.

Image is nestled there, in the very depths of our souls, and our image of ourselves is what causes us to act in the ways we do; it causes us to be who we are at a fundamental level.

Our image is impacted by the people we spend time with, our experiences (positive and negative), decisions, and projections of the future.

The goal of this book is to help you discover some of your beliefs about yourself, and proactively make sure your image is in line with the goals you are setting out to achieve.

As humans, we have this amazing power of metacognition, that is the ability to think about how we think. As Merriam-Webster defines it, metacognition is "the awareness or analysis of one's own learning or thinking processes."

In a nutshell, that means that we can evaluate our thoughts. By processing our thoughts, we can take ownership of them and aim our thoughts, choices, attitudes, and mental trajectories toward the target of our choosing.

It's going to take a lot of work. There will be plenty of trials and errors in the process. There will be plenty of failure. There will be pain, both from growth, and from messing up and dealing with some negative consequences. That is okay. You're not alone in this. This is the human condition.

We can step outside of ourselves and identify key factors that cause us to behave in a certain way or maintain certain habits. That is the first step in effecting change. When we own the image, we own our responses, behaviors, and defining characteristics.

The most important part of this book is *you*. You have to be honest with where you are and what you really think and believe. For the purposes of this book, I can't evaluate you. Your teacher or parent can't evaluate you. This is a self-reflection, and you are the only person who has the answers, the key to yourself, the key to your image.

Feel free to take this book in stages. Ponder it. Apply it to the world around you. If you start to feel overwhelmed, start over from the beginning and take it slowly.

One last thing. It's supposed to be hard. You will not hone your image without a great deal of effort. But it's worth it. And you are worth it!

Write here: I am worth it.

Mean it! I am worth it!

All Caps! I AM WORTH IT!

Three little words, and yet so much about our present and our future is wrapped up in these three words.

Who Am I?

Part of who you are is based on your personality traits and your strengths. It isn't the full picture, but it's one facet.

Write down three personality traits that define you.

Now, write down some of the things you are good at.

> "WE ARE WHAT WE REPEATEDLY DO. EXCELLENCE, THEN, IS NOT AN ACT, BUT A HABIT."
> —WILL DURANT

We are, in part, ourselves because of experiences that we've had, both good and bad.

WHAT ARE TWO EXPERIENCES THAT HAVE DEVELOPED YOU INTO THE SELF THAT YOU CURRENTLY ARE?

GOOD EXPERIENCE

BAD EXPERIENCE

_____   _____

_____   _____

_____   _____

_____   _____

_____   _____

Now, expand on that. Take it deeper. This is where it gets hard. *How* did those experiences impact who you are? How did they make you feel?

That's good. Now we are getting into the real answer to this question, *Who am I?* Keep going. If you don't know the answers to these right away, take time to observe yourself over the course of a week and pay attention; then, make a list.

What motivates you?

1.

2.

3.

What drives you?

1.

2.

3.

What are you willing to skip a meal for or lose sleep for?

1.

2.

3.

What calms you? Is it nature, or something more tangible like a warm hug?

1.

2.

3.

Where do you find peace?

1.

2.

3.

Most of us find strength by practicing a mix of shared experiences with friends and alone time, doing independent activities. What percentage does that look like for you?

Alone   Together

%   %

Draw a picture of something that makes you feel happy, something that makes you feel most like YOU.

You're on your way to creating a good picture for yourself of how you view yourself.

Did You Know?

Your voice sounds different to you than it does to others? Just listen to yourself on camera or on a voicemail. You look different in the mirror to yourself than you look to others when they see you as well.

Have you ever taken a picture with a group of friends and heard someone say "Wait! That's my bad side!" and move before letting someone take their picture?

Most of us are not exactly symmetrical. Part of that is literal differences in the dimensions of our face, but part of it also has to do with our brain and how emotions are displayed. Since much of our emotions are processed in the right side of the brain (the side of the brain that controls the left side of the body), many people have more expressive left sides of their faces, which gives them a not quite symmetrical appearance.

Here is a fun experiment. You can import your picture into the FaceSym app and have it create two faces for you: one that is symmetrical based on your right side, and one that is symmetrical based on your left. Go ahead and try it out!

It's weird, right? It still looks like you, but warped. Did you identify more with one side than the other?

Our inner self is just as diverse as our outer self.

We can be happy people, but still experience moments of deep sadness or depression. We can be kind and caring, and still say or do rude things from time to time; even very selfish people are capable of noble acts.

Each one of us is complex, and to understand ourselves more deeply, we need some more 3D data.

Just as your friends and family see you physically differently than you see yourself, they see you differently as an emotional, intellectual, psychological being as well. We can find out more about who we really are by asking some trusted people in our circle to give us feedback.

On the following pages, you will find a series of prompts for you to fill out, by asking various people for different types of feedback. Some of it will make you feel good and some of it might hurt.

Take this moment to prepare yourself for both the good and the bad. And remember, not everything that hurts us harms us. As a matter of fact, growth is generally painful, but rewarding.

When you are ready to receive the honest feedback of loved ones, people you respect, and friends, move on to the next page and start your interviews.

Remember:

Love yourself completely, even the parts you or others deem "bad." The goal here is for you to collect feedback, consider what others have to say, and then decide for yourself what to do with the information. Don't get offended; don't argue or make excuses. You can repeat back what they are saying to clarify that you have understood their points. Thank them, then ponder the information. You ultimately decide who you want to be and you can make changes as you see fit.

Use this space to write down any fears, concerns, or blocks you have about doing this activity. Acknowledge them, and realize that there is freedom on the other side of fear.

AN ADULT OR A MENTOR WHO HAS KNOWN
YOU FOR A LONG TIME

Name:

How do you know this person?

Ask: In your opinion, what's an experience that shaped me as a person?

A NEW FRIEND

Name:

How do you know this person?

Ask: What are three personality traits that I have that you are drawn to?

Name:

How do you know this person?

Ask: What are two of my worst habits that are going to have long-term consequences?

A SIBLING OR BEST FRIEND

Name:

How do you know this person?

Ask: If I were the Dr. Pepper of personality, what would my primary flavor be?

Now, you've started to construct a meaningful profile of who you are and why you are that way. It might help you understand why you like the things you like, have the friends you have, and struggle with certain things in your life.

If you're thinking, "Gosh. I don't feel good at all right now. There are a lot of parts of me that I don't like," don't worry. We all feel that way. It's like getting your picture taken under a microscope where you see every speck of dirt clogging your pores.

But, we have to get to know ourselves on this level. And we have to accept and love ourselves here, imperfections and all. This is where we are. Throughout the book, we'll discover ways to make necessary changes and to refine the parts of our character that we want to be our strengths.

Right now, we are understanding the bone structure of our character. We can (and we will!) deal with what is most flattering for each one of us individually later on.

So, don't go breaking any bones or being down on yourself for who you are! You need that skeleton, and when we are done refining ourselves, we will each be attractive in our own, unique way.

Who Do I Want to Be?

Before we get into this portion, it's important to clarify that the best person we can be is ourselves. Please, don't feel like you have to imitate someone else or be good at something the way someone else is. That is not the point of this chapter.

Each one of us is going to have different strengths that define us. Some of us are kind or pay attention to details. Others are passionate, physically disciplined, artistic, or great listeners. It's important that we appreciate our differences and do so without attaching a hierarchy to any of them. Smart isn't better than pretty.

Creative isn't better than kind. Passionate isn't better than observant. They all simply *are*, and they provide color, depth, and meaning to life.

PERSONAL EXAMPLE:

When I was younger, I had a friend who was very funny. She always knew the right thing to say at the right time, and everyone loved her for it. When she spoke, people listened.

She would always come up with great one-liners, drop them in the midst of a conversation perfectly, and the entire room would crack up with laughter.

I wanted to be funny, too. More than anything, I wanted to be able to contribute in a meaningful way to conversations.

For a long time, I tried to be funny like my friend. I tried to match her humor and wit, and my jokes and comments would fall hard on the air and make situations uncomfortable.

Fast forward to the present. Sometimes, I am funny. And it's always when I'm not trying. I think it is a skill that I can practice and improve, but it's not the essence of who I am as a person. Instead of trying to match a friend's "funny" or keep up with someone else's humor, I've learned to accept that about the people I spend time with, admire that in them, and enjoy a full-belly laugh when the opportunity presents itself rather than trying to one-up a friend's jokes.

I don't need to be as funny as some of my friends; I am different and contribute in different ways. That's part of why we are friends.

So, if you've been thinking of yourself as better than others because of your unique traits, this is the time to recognize that your traits make you different, but not better than or lesser than others.

We can develop ourselves. We can develop our character. We can develop our personalities. We can evolve. And we do that by establishing a goal and then focusing on our habits.

First, let's define the difference between character and personality.

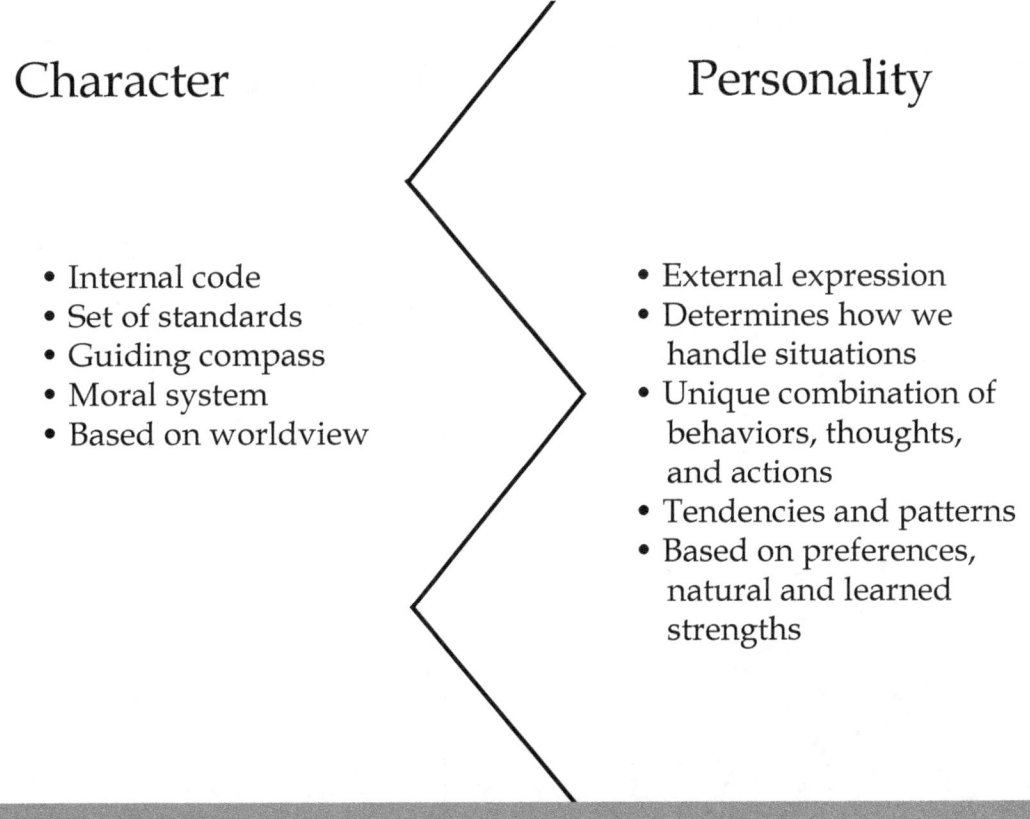

Character

- Internal code
- Set of standards
- Guiding compass
- Moral system
- Based on worldview

Personality

- External expression
- Determines how we handle situations
- Unique combination of behaviors, thoughts, and actions
- Tendencies and patterns
- Based on preferences, natural and learned strengths

Character and personality work together to help us choose our path, and then how to to go about following it. Both of these aspects of ourselves make us unique, not only in their combinations, but in how they play out in real-life situations. That is why you and a friend or family member might share a certain belief, but handle the particulars differently.

Choose the top ten character traits that you find admirable. Then, select seven that you want to incorporate into your life. Here is a very limited list to help get you started, but feel free to brainstorm your own:

- imaginative • thinking outside the box • stoic • determined • persistent
- helpful • aware • kind • open-minded • pensive • generous • comforting
- strong personal boundaries • patient • taking action • calculating the cost/risks
- evaluating • fairness

Make a list of character traits.

1.

2.

3.

4.

5.

6.

7.

8.

9.

10.

Draw a self-portrait below. Then, draw a line from the seven character traits you want to incorporate to your self-portrait. Imagine these traits entering the deepest parts of your being and becoming a part of you.

What are ten personality traits that you admire? Organize these into a new list that is most like you to least like you. Here is a very limited list to help get you started:

• outgoing • private • independent • team-oriented • reliable • intellectual • free-spirited • cultured • courageous • friendly • naive • honest • organized • goal-oriented • confident • cautious • funny • inclusive

MOST LIKE ME

LEAST LIKE ME

Imagine your superhero self. What habits or traits **doesn't** that person have that you have? What **do** they have that you don't? Physical, mental, emotional, psychological, or spiritual traits—any of these count.

Qualities my superhero self has that I want to incorporate:

Struggles, habits, or traits that my superhero self has overcome:

How Am I Going to Get There?

We are going to become the person we want to be through practice, habit formation, and discipline. Habits are to you what gadgets are to superheroes.

Make a list of some awesome superhero gadgets:

Batmobile

Black Panther suit

Iron Man suit

_____

_____

_____

_____

You have to know how to activate and operate these gadgets, or they are useless. Habits have to be planned out, practiced, played out—so that in the heat of the moment, the habit kicks in.

> *Any act often repeated soon forms a habit; and habit allowed, steadily gains in strength.—At first it may be but as the spider's web, easily broken through, but if not resisted it soon binds us with chains of steel.—Tryon Edwards*

We all operate off of our habits. The next time you reach to turn a doorknob, pause. It is your habit that reaches with the left or the right hand. If you try, you can open the door with the other hand. But if you stop thinking about it, you will revert to your habit.

This is true with most of our repetitive behaviors. Left shoe, right shoe or right shoe, left shoe? The way we hold a pencil is a habit. The first tooth touched by your toothbrush is the result of your habit. Fold your arms, clasp your hands, cross your feet at the ankles. There is likely to be a natural, comfortable way to do this. If you reverse the position, it will feel funny. That's habit.

Habits are in place so that we don't have to make conscious decisions about every action in life.

We learn as young people what works for us, and as we mature, we cement those habits. If we want to effect change over a period of time, the best thing we can do is pick out the habit that results in a certain behavior and incorporate the habit.

Some habits are fundamental habits—habits that have a domino effect over other areas of our lives. Charles Duhigg calls these "keystone habits." If you want more information on keystone habits, check out Duhigg's book, *The Power of Habit*.

Keystone habits can be different for different people. This is a time where it is important to reflect on some habits that are keystone habits for you.

Some examples of keystone habits are:

- Doing the dishes right after eating a meal
- Making a list before you sit down to work
- Saving a show as a "treat" for when you are doing cardio or folding/putting away laundry
- Making your bed as soon as you get up in the morning

Three of my keystone habits:

_____

_____

_____

You might not know all of these yet, so if you don't, leave it blank for now. Come back to it after you had a really smooth day, and think about what worked for you.

What did you do?

What did you avoid?

Keep track of those behaviors, and you might be able to trace those good days to a keystone habit that you successfully implemented.

Here are some other questions for you to consider. Circle the ones that apply to you. Do you have a better day if you:

- Shower in the morning versus at night?
- Have coffee versus tea or juice in the morning?
- Exercise in the morning versus the afternoon?
- Do your homework on Friday afternoon versus Sunday afternoon?
- Write your work schedule on a calendar versus in your phone?
- Hang your keys on a hook or put them on a desk/table?

Other things you notice that work better for you:

_____

_____

_____

As we attempt to establish routines and habits that work well for us, it is good to get ideas from other people. Pick someone whom you admire and interview them about their morning routine or, if they're famous, search for their morning routine on the Internet. You don't have to copy this routine, but it always helps to get insight into what is working for others.

After you have spoken with or researched someone else's habits, pick one that you think will be effective and start incorporating it today. Explain the habit and why it will benefit you here:

It's okay to start small. As a matter of fact, it's the only way to start. Pick one thing for now, and be persistent about it. There are a couple of guidelines when it comes to consciously forming a habit that will help you be successful. One way to remember this is to think:

A habit must be PROVEN.

Precise

Reasonable

On a timeline

Visible

Every time

Necessary to achieve an outcome

It takes time and effort to build a habit. If you skip it, you're hurting your future self. That's why your habit has to be PROVEN. Make yourself do it *no matter what* for a month. Be aware that it's going to require sacrifice.

Let's look at this example of creating a habit for someone who always loses their keys.

A nail is pounded into the wall by a door, and the person hangs their keys up immediately after closing the front door.

It's **precise**. There is no question as to where the keys should go.

It's **reasonable** because walking through the door is the first thing this person does when she gets home.

It's **on a timeline**; the keys get hung up before she sets anything else down.

It's **visible**. If the keys aren't there, it's obvious.

It's **every time**. Not just on Mondays and Wednesdays or when she's not in a rush. Every. Time.

It's **necessary in order to achieve the outcome** of saving precious minutes and frustration every time she leaves.

This is a keystone habit because it removes the stress that comes with running late and makes the whole day go more smoothly.

Think about the outcome. What are you trying to accomplish with the new habit? What character trait, personality trait, or life-long goal are you fighting for? Write that down.

_____

_____

Keep that image in your mind. Attach emotion to the image—imagine how you are going to feel when you achieve that outcome. You are going to need all of these motivating factors to push you through the hard times.

Don't quit! If you mess up, stop for a while, or burn out, come back and check this motivation. Start again. Failure is only final if you don't get up and go after your goal after being knocked down.

WHY PUSH THROUGH ALL THIS PAIN?

SO I CAN EXPERIENCE

———————————————

———————————————

(write your motivation here)

The Value of Setting Goals

Goals are hard. They are much harder than dreams. Dreams are ideas that are lofty—brilliant sometimes—but without a foundation. Dreams are sneaky because they sound a lot like goals; but when it comes down to it, they don't have enough substance to make them a reality.

Let's look at a few dreams that look like goals and break them down.

- When I grow up, I'd like to be a great parent.
- I'm going to make a six-figure salary by the time I'm thirty.
- I'm going to exercise and eat better so I can lose some weight.
- I need to study more so that I pass this class!
- I'll get a summer job and save money for travel.

The above examples are all dreams. They are difficult to measure and days go by with no effort on the necessary actions to make these dreams realities.

Let's look at number one.

When I grow up, I'd like to be a great parent.

Define *great parent.* Will it be a list of ten things? Why not eleven? Is a "great parent" of a two-year-old different than a "great parent" of a twelve-year-old?

There's nothing wrong with the dream, per se, but since we don't know the particulars of what the dream actually entails, we can't build toward accomplishing that dream. So, let's turn that dream into a goal.

I want to be a _____, _____, and _____ parent. I want to have a _____ relationship with my children. I want to be _____ and _____ to set a good example for my kids. Most importantly, I want my children to know, above all else, _____.

Example answer: I want to be a <u>kind</u>, <u>patient</u>, and <u>consistent</u> parent. I want to have <u>an honest and open</u> relationship with my children. I want to be <u>approachable</u> and <u>a good communicator</u> to set a good example for my kids. Most importantly, I want my children to know, above all else, <u>that I will be there for them through thick and thin, and that no matter what, they can tell me anything and I'll always love them</u>.

The answers can vary greatly, as can the number of particulars and the focal points. This way of thinking is far more specific than the dream, and we can now break it down into processes and desired outcomes.

Processes are the actions that, over time, will result in a specific outcome. Processes are the behaviors that we choose to turn into habits so that we act in a way that is consistent with the image we are creating.

If we continue on with our "great parent" example, we must identify the processes that we will implement to be this person. You can pick any one of the words that you used to fill in the blank and create a process around this. Here is one as an example.

Kind:

Look for opportunities to do something nice for three people on a daily basis such as:

- Offer to clear someone else's bowl after breakfast
- Raise my hand when my teacher asks for volunteers
- Introduce myself to a new person at school and ask three pleasant questions about their hobbies
- Listen with interest to someone else's story and ask them questions while maintaining focus
- Think before I make jokes and wonder if it might hurt someone

Now, pick a word or phrase you chose and create a list of processes that will help you practice the traits you are attempting to acquire.

_____:

Look for opportunities to _____ on a daily basis such as:

-
-
-
-
-

The third component of these habits is being able to track progress. When we establish the goal and the processes, we must also evaluate some good checkpoints along the way so we make sure we stay on track. This can be as simple as creating a checklist on a phone or a piece of paper and marking when we have accomplished it. We can also keep track of a streak of days where we have met our processes and set up rewards along the way.

Let's look at some checkpoints for our "kind" example.

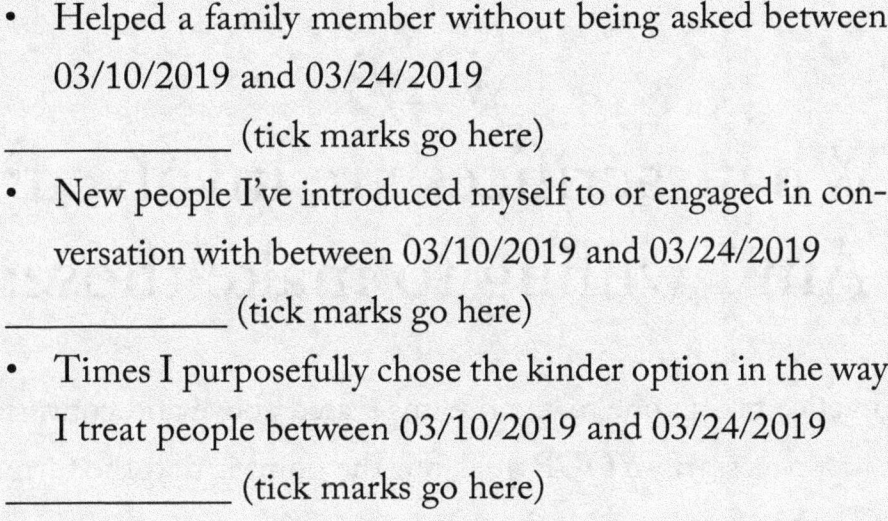

- Helped a family member without being asked between 03/10/2019 and 03/24/2019
  _____ (tick marks go here)
- New people I've introduced myself to or engaged in conversation with between 03/10/2019 and 03/24/2019
  _____ (tick marks go here)
- Times I purposefully chose the kinder option in the way I treat people between 03/10/2019 and 03/24/2019
  _____ (tick marks go here)

Every time we do something we consider "kind," we make a quick tick mark. At the end of this two-week period, we can evaluate what areas we are excelling in and what areas still provide an opportunity for us to grow. We may even find that, after two weeks of practicing mindful kindness, we want to reestablish our checkpoint. That's great! That's why it's a checkpoint, not a destination.

For the sake of differentiating between dreams and goals, let's establish some specifics that will help us create our desired outcomes in a good goal format.

Time Frame:
What needs to happen first?
Then what? Then what? Then what?

Why?
What sacrifices are involved?
Am I willing to make those?

Let's practice taking one of the dreams stated above and converting it into a goal. This isn't necessarily YOUR goal, but the point is that the format works for any goal. Go ahead and try this first one.

I'm going to make a six-figure salary by the time I'm thirty.

We have a time frame in this dream. Next, we need a starting point. Brainstorm (or research) some careers that pay six figures a year.

_____

_____

_____

_____

Now, pick the one that appeals to you most. _____

What is the required expertise and how long does it take? _____

_____

What is the required experience and for how long? _____
_____

Is it available for everyone, or is this for an elite group of people? If it's for an elite group, how are you going to get into that group? _____
_____

Based on this research, what needs to happen first and how long will it take?
_____

Then what? _____
Then what? _____
Then what? _____
Why do I want to make this salary? Go as in-depth as you possibly can. ____

_____

_____

_____

Example answer (not right or wrong, just something for you to compare with):

I'm going to make a six-figure salary by the time I'm thirty.

We have a time frame in this dream. Next, we need a starting point.

Brainstorm (or research) some careers that pay six figures a year.

doctor

successful salesperson

entrepreneur

app designer

Now, pick the one that appeals to you most. entrepreneur

What is the required expertise and how long does it take? Business, marketing, finances, market research, maybe patents… it will take about 3-4 years

What is the required experience and for how long? Experience with a startup, management, business finance, getting investors… 2-4 years

Is it available for everyone, or is this for an elite group of people? If it's for an elite group, how are you going to get into that group? Anyone can do it, but most people fail. It is an elite group of people who are successful. I'd like to get involved in a mentorship program.

Based on this research, what needs to happen first and how can I make that a reality? How long will it take? I need to meet other people who are successful entrepreneurs. I can find local businesses and ask for interviews, see if there are internships or youth programs available in my area, ask counselors, librarians, and teachers if they know anyone they can introduce me to. It will take at least three months to find and meet a couple of successful entrepreneurs who agree to meet with me.

Then what? I need to have questions prepared to ask them.

Then what? I need to take classes on business, marketing, and finances.

Then what? I need to work at a startup company and learn the various roles in the company, both behind the scenes and on the retail side.

Why do I want to make this salary? Go as in depth as you possibly can. <u>I want to make this salary because I want to be able to have a nice home, travel, and feel like I can enjoy certain luxuries without stressing. I want to help my family, charities, and feel like I am a success.</u>

What sacrifices are involved? Am I willing to make those? <u>I will have to sacrifice a lot of free time to be researching companies, contacting people, writing questions, and interviewing those people. I will have to be prepared that many people might not be willing to meet with me. I will have to sacrifice money and time to take classes to prepare me. I'll have to choose a job that will train me to be an entrepreneur, and I might have to start at the bottom of the totem pole. I am not willing to make these sacrifices just for money, but I might be if I really believe in the business I start or the product/service I provide.</u>

Were your answers similar? Completely different? Ask a friend, classmate, or parent to answer these questions and compare your answers with theirs.

Turn it into a goal.

Now that we have this wealth of information, we can turn it into a goal. Let's make sure we incorporate all the items from our goal-creation checklist:

Time frame

What needs to happen first?

Then what?

Then what?

Then what?

Why?

What sacrifices are involved? Am I willing to make those?

By the time I'm thirty, I'll have a job as _____ that pays me a six-figure salary. I will _____, _____ _____, and _____ _____ in order to be prepared to _____ _____ _____. I am willing to give up _____, spend money on _____, and _____ in order to _____ _____.

Example answer:

By the time I'm thirty, I'll have a job as <u>an entrepreneur</u> that pays me a six-figure salary. I will <u>meet mentors and other business owners, take classes in marketing, business, and finances, and work at a startup company to learn the ins and outs of the business</u> in order to be prepared to <u>have a role that provides enough money for me and my family to experience luxuries such as travel and a nice home, as well as have enough to share with others</u>. I am willing to give up <u>free time</u>, spend money on <u>education</u>, and <u>work my way up the ladder</u> in order to <u>offer a product or service that adds value.</u>

Whew! That was exhausting. And, that's only the beginning. Now, we actually have to do the work! But what we just did is **the main reason many people leave their desired outcomes in the field of dreams.** It is mentally taxing to create a real goal, to write it down on paper, and to come to grips with the work, sacrifices, and difficulties that are bound to come along with an established goal.

Pick one of the following dreams and repeat the process again to convert the dream into a goal. Better yet, skip these stock dreams if one doesn't apply to you and make your own! The more you practice, the easier it gets!

- I'm going to exercise and eat better so I can lose some weight.
- I need to study more so that I pass this class!

- I'll get a summer job and save money for travel.
- My dream: _____

Time frame_____

Next, we need a starting point:

Brainstorm (or research) some places to start.

_____

_____

_____

_____

Now, pick the one that appeals to you most. _____

What is the required expertise and how long does it take? _____

_____

What is the required experience and for how long? _____

_____

Is it available for everyone, or is this for an elite group of people? If it's for an elite group, how are you going to get into that group? _____

_____

Based on this research, what needs to happen first and how long will it take?

_____

Then what? _____

Then what? _____

Then what? _____

Why do I want to do this? Go as in depth as you possibly can. _____

_____

_____

_____

_____

Whew! Now, ready to make this a goal?

By_____(time frame), I'll _____
_____ (final outcome). I will _____,
_____, and _____
(do these three things) in order to be prepared to _____
_____ because _____
_____ (what and the reasons behind the why). I am willing
to give up _____, do _____, and
_____ (another action verb) in order to _____
_____ (active role in the desired outcome).

When we are setting goals, determining the actions we will take, and establishing new routines and habits, it is good for us to keep track of our consistent efforts. We can call the consistent efforts over a given number of days our "streak." For example, if your goal is to keep track of your meals on your phone through a given app, you can see how many days in a row you have logged in to your app. That number of days is your streak. If you are working on reading a book for thirty minutes per day, each day in a row you accomplish that counts toward your streak.

We can use this chart to organize our outcomes, processes, and checkpoints or timeline:

Outcome   Processes   Checkpoint

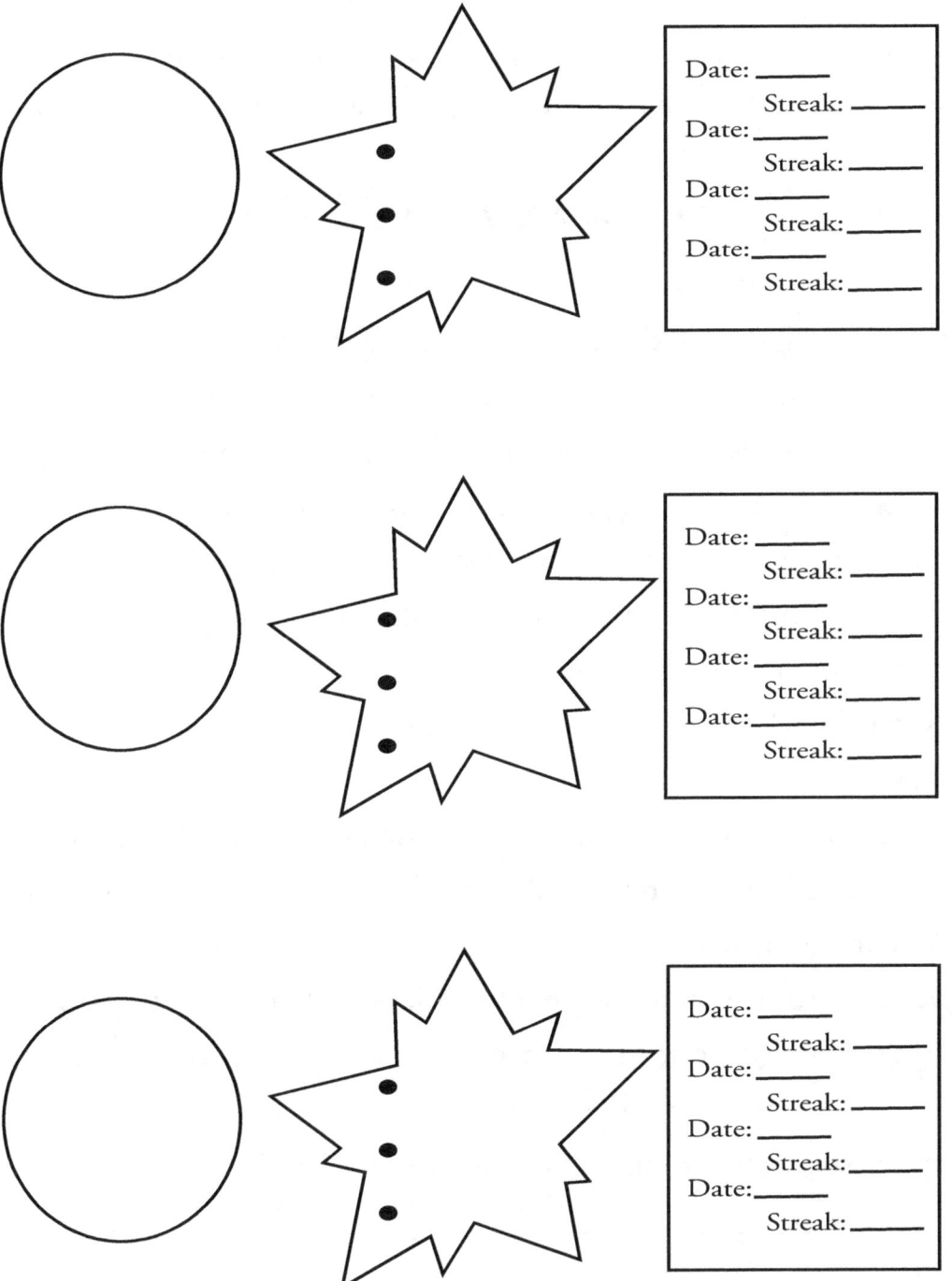

HINT:

It's important to focus on one to three things at a time. As you just went through the agony of the mental exhaustion that comes from changing the way you think, it's important to recognize that we can't change ourselves all at once. Pick a couple of goals, determine the processes, and focus on those for a given time period. When those habits are solid, then start the process again with new goals.

Strive, Struggle, Evolve!

It's supposed to be hard.

While that might sound like an awful thing to say, it really isn't. It should make you feel relieved and recognize that this is hard for everyone.

Imagine that you want to get stronger. You decide to lift weights. So, you pick up your pencil and start doing bicep curls. Think anything is going to happen? Do you imagine there will be much growth taking place?

Of course not! It has to be a challenge. It has to be hard enough to push you, but not hard enough to break you.

Let's start by taking this one word at a time.

STRIVE.

Strive is a beautiful word that implies desire, stretch, mindset, and focus; it's when something is doable, but it's difficult. Think standing on your tippy toes to reach an item on the highest shelf.

Strive can also be a more noble undertaking. Olympians strive to break records. Singers and dancers strive to give a spotless performance. Researchers strive to find the truth about the facts of history.

What are some other examples of people who strive?

_____

_____

We actively participated in striving when we set our goals. It is hard to put the ideas down on paper, force the concepts into words, and refine them into the essence of a goal.

After we set our aim, it is time for the next phase.

STRUGGLE.

Struggle is a word we might not particularly like. Generally, people try to avoid struggle. It isn't comfortable, and it isn't generally efficient. It is, however, a necessary component of growth.

The whole point of setting goals is to move from A to B, to excel, to grow. Any time there is change or movement, there is guaranteed to be a struggle.

Due to the nature of work, effort has to be exerted in order to get any sort of productivity. Without getting too scientific here, this is true on a physical level as well as on a mental level. Just as you will have to push your body against resistance in order to grow more muscle, you will have to push yourself mentally in order to grow a new habit.

It's important to know what the struggle looks like so we can be prepared to push through it when necessary.

Let's take our "six-figure salary by thirty" for example. As we fleshed this dream out into a real goal, we also noted some education and experience requirements, as well as sacrifices that would be necessary in achieving this goal.

What are some of the struggles that might come up as a result of the education requirement?

Finding a job that works around your class schedule

_____

_____

What are some of the struggles that might come up as a result of the experience requirement?

Knowing how to write a good resume

_____

_____

We talked about sacrifices of both time and money. How might those play out into *struggles*?

Missing a spring break trip because of finances tied up in saving for an education

_____

_____

Struggles never look good. As a matter of fact, they look a whole lot like failure. Keep pushing through anyway. Failure is only final when you give up.

Some areas in my life where I have had struggles or failures:

_____

_____

_____

_____

The next part of the process is the fun part, but it's the part that takes the most time.

Evolve.

The word *evolve* is such a cool word because it implies slow, almost unnoticeable changes over an extended period of time.

Think of a flower blooming. It is first a stem, a bud, a bulb, then finally a bloom.

Think of yourself as a child. One year. Two. Then three. Somewhere along the line, your hair grew. You acquired a vocabulary. You established preferences in foods and toys. You grew taller. You got all your teeth.

While habits are focused implementations of processes that will deliver the desired results, the results take a while to bloom. And generally, it doesn't happen all at once.

Let's say a goal was to create a travel savings account by giving up unnecessary dining out expenses. The first time you forego your coffee at Starbucks, you might feel a little discouraged. After all, it only saved you four dollars.

(Enter the struggle.) "This is stupid. It's so not worth it. It's only four dollars that I'm saving, and four dollars isn't going to get me anywhere I want to go. I should just get the coffee today and find a better way to save money." (Warning! You are in the midst of making a decision in the moment rather than following the process. Follow the process!)

Whew. You made it. It was hard, but you successfully skipped Starbucks and now have four dollars in your savings account. After you do this a few times, that money will start to grow. It will slowly accumulate.

Over six months, you might save around $200. It's slow, but it's a start. When you combine that with the several meals you didn't eat in restaurants, the popcorn you forewent at the movies twice, you're now at a whopping $425—enough to buy a plane ticket to almost anywhere in the U.S.

But, it takes time.

It takes time for our character to evolve as well. If we are trying to establish awareness or attentiveness in our surroundings so that we can be more useful at our jobs, it will take time for us to fully acquire that skill.

It takes time for new pathways to form in our brain. Repetitive, focused action is necessary as we first start to cut new paths in our consciousness. Think of taking a stick through mud or sand. The first time you drag the stick, it has no rule, no guide. After the first path is made, you can go over it again and again, making it deeper, wider, more permanent.

As the path evolves, so do we as we create a trajectory, repeat the process, and form a deeply ingrained habit.

In all of this evolving, it is extremely important that we maintain an attitude of gratitude. While it is crucial to keep our sights on the goal of what we want to accomplish, we also have to find ways to be grateful for the present.

We must love ourselves as we are, accept where we are, and be patient with ourselves in the growth process.

Gratitude can be expressed by keeping a list of things that have gone right, such as finding a close parking spot on a rainy day or discovering that a friend saved you a seat when you were running late.

It's good to write these things down, because when the dark times come, you can look at your list and be reminded that there have also been times of light and joy. Our memories tend to forget these little moments or we forget to focus on being grateful for the joys in life. A list will help keep those positive moments present in our minds.

Gratitude can be practiced informally throughout the day, too. When the sun's rays hit your skin, close your eyes and smile in the warmth for a moment. Savor the first bite of a warm meal or the first sip of a fresh cup of coffee, and be grateful. Thank a friend or a loved one for their support and for caring. Take a walk through a greenhouse or a park and stop and appreciate the flowers.

Keep an attitude of gratitude. Be present, and be thankful.

Taking this positive vibe with us throughout our day helps us not only to anchor our emotions, but it also helps us be more aware of the positive opportunities around us. As we are attentive to good things, we literally see other good things that have been there all along that we just hadn't noticed before.

It's worth it to take several moments a day to practice purposeful gratitude. What are some things you are grateful for?

The Power of the Checklist

Have you ever had a thought of something you wanted for Christmas or your birthday, and then forgotten what it was when someone asked you what you wanted? Have you had something that you knew needed to get done, and then you completely spaced doing it? Have you been to the store only to get home and realize you forgot a crucial item?

In situations like these, the checklist comes in handy. Whether your checklist is in a journal, on a piece of paper, on your phone notes, or even in a text message to you or someone else, it is valuable to have a place to quickly jot down information when it comes to mind. Not only does it help you do the things you meant to do, but it also takes that burden of remembering off your mind, freeing up working memory and brain power that you can dedicate to something else.

The checklist is a simple tool that we can incorporate in other areas of our lives as well, especially when we are forming a new habit. You can call your checklist a checklist, a formula, or the steps to success, but it must be orderly, clear, and broken into minute details.

Let's look at how we can use a checklist to help us in habit formation.

Perhaps you are looking to have a better school year by having a more organized backpack. Your goal is to keep your papers and assignments where you can find them when you need them, and make sure that old oranges, chocolate bars, and cheese sticks don't live for months moldering in the bottom of your backpack. Great idea!

It's likely that every person who gets a new backpack or throws out last year's leftover papers and forgotten items (that orange, though… eek!) decides to "be more organized this year."

A few weeks into the school year, there are crumpled papers, broken pencils, and some snack that is well on its way to fermentation. That's because "be more organized this year" is a _____, not a _____.

What we need is a goal, a habit, and a checklist.

Goal

Habit

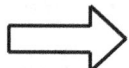

Checklist

Sometimes, it's easier to attach new habits to the end of other habits that we already have. It helps us do it consistently. Let's first establish what our current habits are, then find a way to attach a habit that will help us meet our goal.

After school/work, I arrive at home at _:__.

The first thing I do when I walk in the door is _____ _____.

Next, I _____ and _____ _____.

Some of my evening responsibilities include _____, _____, and _____.

Two habits I need to incorporate into my daily routine in order to accomplish my organizational goal are _____ and _____.

Based on this routine, the best time to incorporate those habits is right before or after I _____.

Some situations when I won't be able to do this are _____ and _____.

I will account for these times that I will miss by doing _____ _____.

It's easy to get down on yourself if you can't do something every day. The negative voice in your mind can start telling you that it isn't even worth it to try when you aren't going to be able to go all out. Shut that voice down. By keeping a checklist, you will be able to keep track of progress over a week or a month. Even if you don't do sit-ups every day, doing them

The habits you choose to create don't have to feel good, they just have to benefit your life to make room for the things you love and are passionate about; they are there to propel you closer to your goals and dreams.
-Jadi Stuart

Behold, The Power of 15 minutes

three times a week is better than not doing them at all.

There are many things in life like this; exercise, scheduling, cleaning, and preparation for the next day might not be things you can get to *every day*. But doing what you can prevents major build up over the long term.

Fifteen minutes doesn't seem like a lot of time. It's certainly easy to waste fifteen minutes. It's easy to watch fifteen minutes of a show you aren't even that into when you're plopped in front of the TV. Fifteen minutes is more or less the time it takes to listen to four songs, the time it takes for chocolate chip cookies to bake in the oven, and the amount of time it takes to walk half a mile. Technically, if you planned it just right, you could do all of these things at the same time. You could put the cookies in the oven, grab your headphones, and do a brisk fifteen-minute walk before pulling the cookies out of the oven to cool. (I only recommend this if there is a responsible adult in the house; you never want to leave the oven while unattended.)

Sometimes, when it seems like the workload in front of you seems overwhelming and undoable, set your timer for fifteen minutes and dedicate yourself to working on a particular project for just that amount of time. When the timer goes off, you get to quit whether or not the work is done. You'll be surprised just how much you can get done in fifteen dedicated minutes.

Try these out and see which list you are able to accomplish in a fifteen-minute window (with no distractions!) Silence your phone, turn off the TV, cut the music and just get in the zone of your project.

CLEAN UP PHYSICAL HABITAT

Make the bed.
Vaccuum your room.
Start a load of laundry.
Wipe down the toilet.
Sweep the bathroom.
Straighten your bathroom towel.

15 MINUTES

Deal with Clutter

Open your mail.

Delete 15 old emails that are taking up space.

Plug in all devices that need charged (headphones, tablets, computers, etc.)

Wipe down your desk or homework workspace with disinfectant.

Straighten your shoes.

Clear off a shelf and toss unnecessary items.

Dust the shelf off before putting anything back.

15 MINUTES

FOCUS ON PHYSICAL STRENGTH

Do 25 crunches.
Do 25 pushups.
Do 25 jumping jacks.
Do 15 lunges on each leg.
Do 15 squats.
Stretch your back, legs, and arms.

Learn About a Relevant topic

Read a magazine article or an educational article on LinkedIn or Twitter.
Look up two words in the dictionary or find a synonym on the Internet.
Write a list of pros and cons about the arguments presented in the article.
Write a response or a journal entry about the topic. Date it.

15 MINUTES

BE PEACEFUL AND DESTRESS

Listen to ocean waves or mountain breezes while you focus on controlled breathing.

Verbalize three things you are grateful for.

Envision the changing of the seasons from spring to summer to fall to winter.

Recognize that we go through seasons as well.

Remind yourself that this too will pass.

Imagine the sun on your skin, the wind on your face, and the sounds and colors of nature.

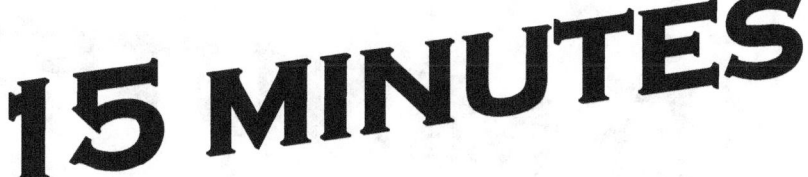

15 MINUTES

What else?

-
-
-
-
-
-

15 MINUTES

It's also helpful to have a running checklist of things to do when you don't know what to do. This might be for when you are waiting for the rest of the class to finish a test, when someone is running late to a meeting, when your ride isn't ready to go yet, or when you are waiting in the doctor's office or the Department of Motor Vehicles (DMV). It's tempting to scroll through a social media platform (not that that's bad, but it can become a time waster). Think of some other things you could do with a handful of spare minutes.

5-10 minutes at home, waiting for your ride

_____

_____

_____

5-10 minutes after a test or before a meeting

_____

_____

_____

15-30 minutes in an office waiting room

_____

_____

_____

"The person who masters the minute rules the day."
- Unknown

Everything you can do while you are waiting will help you accumulate blocks of time to dedicate to accomplishing the big goals you defined earlier in this book. Master those minutes, and see just how much you can accomplish in your day.

The trick here is to already have a checklist ready to go. When you have five minutes, you might look around for two minutes trying to figure out what to do, then use one minute motivating yourself to do it, and by the time you start, two minutes isn't really enough to complete the task. Instead, *if you will dedicate some time to having a checklist ready,* you can immediately jump into action and start on the task at hand.

Discipline

What does "having discipline" or "being disciplined" mean to you? _____
_____

What is the hardest part for you when it comes to doing something consistently? Is it time, remembering to do it, desire, or something else? Dig deep here to discover *what* is keeping you from following through on the necessary actions to accomplish your goals.

_____
_____
_____

Implied in the word "discipline" is a sense of self-control, withholding from yourself something you want, or even using a form of restraint to keep yourself within certain boundaries.

There are different levels of discipline motivated by different things. Our bodies tend to respond to punishment on different levels, based on our age, maturity, and the things that matter to us.

Personal Example:

In the basement in the home where I grew up, we had a cement floor painted a deep, hunter green. It had a small sitting area arranged where a wood-burning stove used to be before we had central heating in the house.

One day, I was playing with one of my good friends, and I got extremely angry at my mom. I don't remember why now (imagine that... all that emotional energy wasted on something I forgot about), but I was livid.

On a side table in the sitting area was a bodacious peach lamp—a lamp my mom really liked—complete with a forest green lampshade. Its gold cord trailed from its base like the sleek tail of an animal, and all I could think about was smashing that lamp against the green cement.

I went so far as to unplug it. I imagined the sound of the lamp as the glass shattered, the garbled sound the lampshade would make as it bent against the floor. I thought of the shards of glass spraying in a thousand directions, and was excited by the sheer destructiveness of breaking my mom's lamp.

Before I took that lamp in my hands to smash it, I thought of two things: the punishment consequences, and how the outrageous behavior would make me look in the eyes of my friend.

The consequences of what would happen in the aftermath of the outburst would be bad. I would have to clean up the mess (which would result in a full floor sweeping) and do extra work around the house to pay back the value of the lamp. It would take me only seconds to destroy the lamp, but lots of time paying the consequences. The thought of those consequences made me stop and evaluate before I shattered the lamp.

Trying to avoid negative consequences was one form of discipline that worked to control my behavior. The other component that impacted my choice was the thought of maintaining the respect of my friend. The image or expectation that I wanted to maintain in her eyes was a second form of restraint for me, a social restraint that, in a sense, disciplined my behavior.

Most of us try to avoid painful punishments, especially when we are convinced that we are going to be caught. It is why rules generally work. If a police officer catches us speeding, it is painful to pay the expensive ticket. If we don't follow the rules at our pool or gym, we can get kicked out and not be allowed to return.

Punishment-based disciplines are likely the simplest and quickest forms of discipline, but rarely are they the most effective. Punishment creates fear of the punishment, not necessarily a desire to change the behavior.

We talk about punishments here when we are looking into the topic of self-discipline because it's important that we approach image change in a positive way. If we aren't careful, we can end up creating self-loathing even with the greatest of intentions.

Let's check out a couple of examples.

EXAMPLE:

Aby has a goal to lose twenty pounds. She forgets to pack a lunch because she is running late, so by the time she gets to Gayle's birthday party, she's starving. She eats three pieces of pizza and two cupcakes, then immediately feels bad. What went wrong?

Aby might have a self-discipline weakness when it comes to food. Or Aby might have a weakness of preparing ahead of time. Aby should:

a. sit in front of the mirror and pinch her fat rolls while saying "I'm a pig."

b. force herself to go on a three-mile run, even if she's not in shape for it, and skip a meal the next day.

c. call her best friend and cry, explaining why she hates herself.

d. eat a pint of ice cream to top off the day. After all, it was already a major fail.

e. acknowledge that she messed up and figure out *why* she ate as much as she did. She should then focus her energy on a plan for the next day that will help her reach her weight-loss goal.

Add a step to the right answer. What else should Aby do as a part of her reflective self-discipline?_____

_____

_____

EXAMPLE:

Thierry has been having difficulties with letting go of his last relationship. He has been obsessing about his ex, checking out all of her posts on social media to see who she is with, texting her after she has asked him to stop, and trying to get information from her friends and acquaintances about what she is doing. He knows this is crossing a boundary, but he's having a hard time disciplining himself to respect her boundaries. What should Thierry do?

Thierry might have a self-discipline weakness when it comes to working through his emotions and feelings. Thierry should:

a. recognize that he's a loser and that no one is ever going to like him again. He should give up on her, and give up on relationships all together.

b. find someone else as a rebound. After all, if she didn't like the fact that he was crazy about her, maybe she will be jealous when she sees him giving all that attention to someone else.

c. make a list of all the things he hated about his ex and post it on social media. She wasn't worth his time anyway, and he's got dirt on her that will embarrass her.

d. hurt himself physically. After all, when she sees how bad he's hurting, she'll have to come back.

e. evaluate what it was about the relationship that he misses so badly. Was it the company? The physical affection? Someone special he could look forward to seeing every day? He should try to figure out what need that relationship was filling for him and try to find other ways to feed his soul. In the meantime, he should focus his attention on doing positive, helpful things that will be a favor for his future self. Exercise, spending time on a hobby or project, helping his family, or reconnecting with his guy friends will help him get distance from the emotional turmoil of the breakup.

Add a step to the right answer. What else should Thierry do as a part of his self-discipline in respecting his ex's boundaries? _____
_____
_____

Try this yourself. Think of something you have been working on that you have had discipline struggles with. Write it out, then we'll come up with some various ways of handling the issue. Pick something small to begin!

I've been struggling with _____. Even when I know I should _____, I can't seem to help but _____ instead. I think the biggest problem is _____
_____.

Now, think about punishments, rewards, and outcomes. We are going to write down options, both good and bad, so that we can verbalize some things our minds do to trick us when we are struggling with discipline.

a. (write something self-deprecating here that we can agree is ridiculous)

b. (write something extreme here that might feel good for a moment, but won't feel good in the long term)

c. (make an excuse here that has some truth to it, but that isn't a real solution)

d. (write something here that will cause hurt, but also feel good in a warped way because it plays into feelings of guilt)

e. (write out the best, mature solution that will help you start where you are at and make positive gains from here on out)

Add a step to the right answer. What else should you do as a part of creating a viable solution to the struggles you are having? _____ _____ _____

Develop Your Self-Confidence

Think of self-confidence as it comes to goals, habits, and checklists as a game of golf.

Everyone wants to hit a hole in one. It rarely happens. Instead, you hit the ball off the tee in the general direction of where you want it to go.

Sometimes you miss the ball entirely. Swing again.

Sometimes the ball looks like it's going in the perfect direction and then it suddenly curves and rolls into the trees, the sand, or the rough. Work your way back onto the green. It may take a few hits. Keep progressing.

Sometimes you are set up for a perfect putt into the hole and you overhit or underhit. Breathe, focus, and leave the past behind you. Hit the ball into the hole.

Remember, there are eighteen holes in golf. Repeat.

In life, you will likely experience these phases through all of the habits you try to create. Over time, you will get better at the process of habit formation and follow-through. The good news is, you have many more than eighteen "holes" or opportunities at new habits in life.

Every habit you form now helps you with future ones by extending your experience, shining a light on your weaknesses, highlighting your strengths, and bolstering your confidence as you make gains.

It is crucial to start small. Build a pattern of success. Walk, then run.

We all need a little motivation sometimes. Encouragement, support, and reassurance are some of our deepest needs. Ideally, it's great to have someone or a group of people who are able to help you during your lowest times. Unfortunately, each of us will go through some hard times where it is impossible for others to give us enough support.

In times like this, we must dig deep within ourselves and decide that we will be okay, even if we aren't right now. Keep in mind that this too will pass. Remember that the way you feel right now won't be a forever feeling: no feeling, good or bad, lasts forever.

USE THIS CHART WHEN YOU ARE STRUGGLING WITH YOUR SELF-CONFIDENCE.

What's the general direction of this "swing?"

_____

_____

What does the "rough" look like in the context of the habit I'm trying to build? _____

_____

_____

_____

Where is "the ball" currently at? The rough? The green? Explain:

_____

_____

_____

I've experienced some setbacks, and I'm disappointed that this wasn't a hole-in-one. Setbacks:

_____

_____

_____

Here are three things I can do to start getting myself back on track.

_____

_____

_____

Find a list of quotes, pictures, songs, or reminders that help you feel better. While you are compiling that list for yourself, there is an excellent compilation of inspiring quotes by Peter Economy that you can find online to serve as the kindling for the fire of your own self-curated list of motivations.

Remember:

It takes a while to get out of the rough. Keep swinging. Now, use your self-discipline to make yourself carry out the three actions that will help you get back on track.

Do you ever wonder why things can't just be easier? Why does "the rough" have to exist, anyway?

The answer circles back around to growth. Challenges are the only things that make us grow. We have to strive for something that is hard, struggle until we master the process, and evolve into the person who can successfully accomplish the thing we set out striving for.

We can stop after that. The problem is that when we stop striving, we lose our "why"—our sense of purpose that makes life worth living.

The challenges in life, or the "rough," is there so that we keep on playing the game. There is an amazing feeling after we successfully make it through the challenges, and we learn about our strength, tenacity, and our ability to rise to the occasion.

So, if you're feeling down about the struggle, if you feel like you are stuck in the rough and can't get out, take heart. We've all felt that way. You can get out of it, but you have to keep on struggling until you gain the strength in yourself to evolve.

One day, you'll look back on these hard times and think, "Wow. I never thought I was going to make it through that, and look. I did. I can get through this next challenge as well."

Keep track of your successes and use them to bolster you into the next round of challenges. You've been through tough things before and survived. You can face whatever is coming at you!

Reevaluate Periodically

One of the reasons we have checkpoints along the way in our habits is to make sure we are staying on track. Another reason for these checkpoints is to make sure the path we are on is indeed the right path to take us to our goals.

When we reevaluate, we provide ourselves with the option to make changes and improvements along the way. If we have been working on using our study time wisely, but don't see any improvement in our progress report or midterm grades, we need to evaluate what is being effective and what isn't.

Checkpoints don't generally get to happen as soon as we would like them to. If you go to the gym for one day and weigh yourself immediately after, you will discover that your weight hasn't changed, and the problem is not with the process. The problem is with the timing. If you follow the process and weigh in at three weeks and don't see any positive change, it might be time to reevaluate the process. You might look into your diet, sleep, water intake, and effectiveness of exercise. Tweak what you can, and follow the process for another three weeks.

It's important to set up our evaluations at appropriate times. If we wait all semester to have a grade checkpoint, it may be too late. If we don't check our savings figure to make sure that money is accumulating until it's time to buy the ticket, we may be too late.

The goal with reevaluation is to assess where we are at, keep the good habits we have started, and make refinements as necessary.

Let's take a look at the dream we turned into a goal on page thirty-one:

By_____(timeframe), I'll _____
_____ (final outcome). I will _____,
_____, and _____
_____ (do these three things) in order to be prepared to _____
_____ because _____
_____ (what and the reasons behind the why). I am willing to give up _____, do _____, and
_____ (another action verb) in order to _____
_____ (active role in the desired outcome).

Now, let's establish some checkpoints that will serve to make sure our habits are helping us reach this desired outcome.

What's a reasonable timeline for checkpoints in a year span? _____
_____

List three things that are measurable that you can use as feedback. (This might look like number of applications filled out, weight change, assignments turned in, chores done, etc.)

_____

_____

_____

Try this chart again with specific dates where you will evaluate your processes and the measurable gains:

Outcome   Processes   Checkpoint

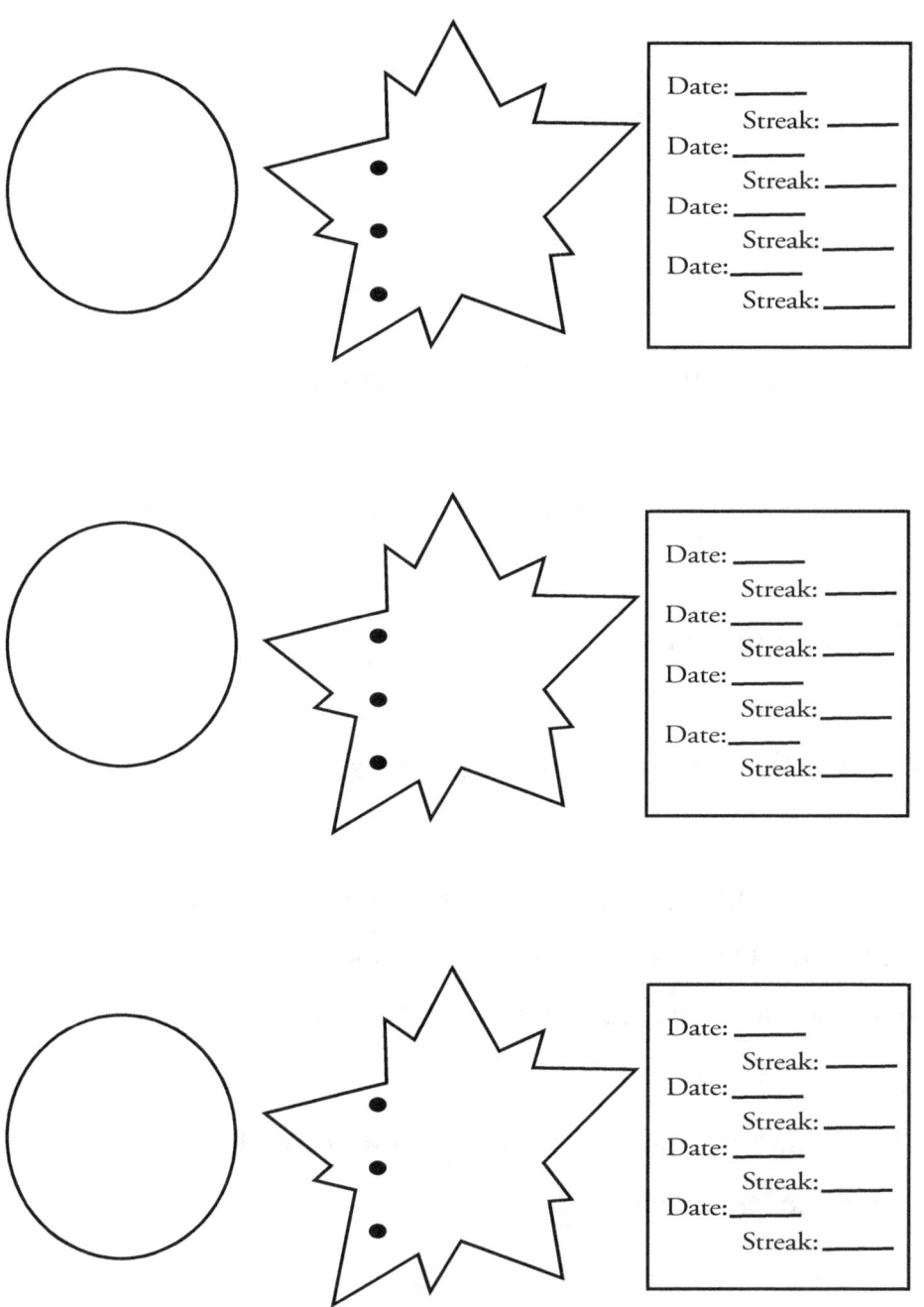

Assess your progress.

- Have I followed the process consistently?

- When and where did I drop off?

- What did I do to get back on track?

- Do I see any noticeable gains?

- What's keeping me from being more consistent in my habits?

- Is the process going to produce the results that I want?

- What can I do to make this process 5% better?

- What kind of motivation can I incorporate to help me be more committed?

- Is there something I can use as a sort of safety net reminder? (i.e. no video games until I've organized my backpack or no changing into sweats until I've completed my assignments for the day)

- What is just flat-out not working? How can I keep the good parts and change the less effective ones?

This revision process is not a one-time thing. Every time you hit a checkpoint, you need to revisit this evaluation procedure. It will help you make sure you are staying on track, and that the track you are on is the right track for where you are currently at.

Collect Feedback, and Know What to Do With It

If we listen and observe with an open mind, we will get feedback from those around us. Sometimes, people will say things and other times we can learn what they think from their body language.

Friends, family members, teachers, classmates, coaches, bosses, co-workers, and people we don't get along with are all viable sources of feedback. While it is important to be sure of ourselves and not rely solely on others' perceptions of us, we can collect feedback and put it under the microscope of our own perspective later.

Getting feedback is a mature process, and it requires maturity to accept it. After all, you're putting your best out there and offering someone else a scalpel to cut into the parts of you that aren't smooth or that need adjusting.

DON'T GET
DEFENSIVE

This is easier said than done.

Don't

- **Expect that you won't get any negative feedback.** You are not perfect right out of the gate; the purpose of getting feedback is for you to be able to improve over time until the critiques have been resolved.

- **Beat yourself up**. Cry and experience the pain for a short time, then get back to work! If you can get criticism on paper, you can use the goal-setting system in this book to help resolve the weaknesses. It will take time, but your final product will be significantly improved.

- **Get huffy and tell someone that they clearly didn't understand you**. If they didn't understand, chances are someone else will have the same difficulty. Ask them how you could communicate the point you were trying to make more clearly.

- **Explain under the guise of making excuses**. Listen and ask questions.

- **Avoid someone's comments**. Thank them for being honest and sharing their opinion with you, even if you silently disagree.

Do

- Tell people how you want them to formulate their feedback.
- Give a guide as to what exactly you want feedback on.
- Ask people to tell you both strengths and places for improvement.
- Listen to their perspective without forming an argument for your side.
- Ask for clarification. "So, let me see if I'm hearing you correctly. You're saying…" is a great phrase.
- Ask questions and offer alternatives. "Would it be better if I did/said/ approached the situation like this?"
- Thank the person for their honest feedback.

REMEMBER:

In the polishing process,
we use several different
grits of sand and multiple passes.
No one is polished
without the process of multiple revisions
through constructive criticism!

Choose Your Own Unique Culture

No one has figured out the exact right way to do everything. Part of the reason is that there are so many perfectly acceptable ways to accomplish the same outcomes. At times, it comes down to personal preference or taste. And it's okay to switch it up.

Food is a good example of this. Mexican? Italian? Mediterranean? What about a good ol' burger? All of these meet the goal of sustaining our bodies' energy. Some days you might be in the mood for an Indian meal, and other times you might really want Chinese takeout. You are allowed to have a mix of styles of preparation that you enjoy to satisfy your need for food.

The same is true for the way you choose to do things. As there are seasons in nature, we have seasons in our lives. Some seasons are more productive than others. Some seasons are more about reflection. You get to choose how you go about incorporating a mix of various ways of doing things so that it works with your lifestyle.

There is a modern phenomenon of watching YouTube personas play video games. It is a huge, monetized industry. (Yes. Watching someone else play a game via the Internet is bringing in the big bucks.) It seems absurd at first, but as we delve in a little deeper, perhaps we can gain a better understanding. Video games are fun for many people, and the best games are complicated and difficult. Succeeding at these games is easier when you know what is coming ahead; it allows your mind the opportunity to have an image of what to expect rather than being surprised by the unknown. Not only do you get to see the next phase of the game, but you get to see someone successfully accomplish the feat while, at times, explaining what is happening and demonstrating some of the tricks in the game that will help you be successful.

Life is not that much different. It is valuable to interact with people in a variety of age ranges, cultures, backgrounds, and social situations because they have been through parts of "the game" that you haven't traversed yet. By observing how these other people respond to situations or adapt to problems, you can learn how to get through your own course more successfully.

Be curious. Ask questions when you see someone having success in a particular area or when you desire similar outcomes.

Maybe you're struggling with your grades in a subject and you want to see how people who are getting As in the class are studying. Ask them to show you their binders or study schedules.

Some topics that might be of interest are:

Jobs

Finances

Creative endeavors

Girls

Boys

Building supportive friendships

Dealing with family issues, such as divorce

Athletics

Planning for college

Setting boundaries with siblings

_____

_____

_____

Sometimes, it's easier to step into good habits and maintain them if you already have someone else who is doing the same thing (or something similar) who can show you the way or go alongside you as you incorporate something new into your life. This is why a gym buddy or study group can help everyone involved do better; not only is the other person counting on you and motivating you, but you are collectively benefiting from each others' strength.

One of the most important concepts that we must take with us as we consider our image, goals, and desired outcomes is that this is a constant, evolutionary process. You will not finish this book and be done with your quest for self-improvement. It is only the beginning. There is no "I have arrived!" moment where you discover that you have become your perfect self. It is, rather, a continual process of self-development that carries on as your worldview expands and as your understanding of self gets richer and more intricate.

May you strive, struggle, and evolve!

ACKNOWLEDGMENTS

There is no such thing as a perfect rough draft, and with regards to this book, there would be no final draft were it not for the crucial input of several wonderful people.

Erika Vargas Estrada, Cherie Ferguson, Mary-Ellen Gomez, Lauren Klemke, Mark Schultz, and Jadi Stuart, your time, effort, comments, and revisions are greatly appreciated. Thank you for being a huge part of this book!

Erin Huebener and Lori Shanahan, thank you for allowing me to bounce ideas off of you, for always giving me your honest opinion, and for believing in social progress.

Aunt Cherie, thank you for being supportive of this series, and of my books in general. Your comments and edits have been so helpful for the past five years worth of writing! Here's to five more.

Danny Doyle, thank you for asking the difficult questions pertaining to real-world application and for always bringing my thoughts out of the clouds and into the practical.

Vanessa Flores, cover designer extraordinaire! Thank you for a beautiful concept for the series and for the many FaceTime calls, Photoshop guide lessons, and conversations that make a collaborative effort enjoyable.

Thank you to the hyper-speller Mark Schultz, AKA Word Refiner, for your constant support and belief in this series. Your keen eyes and consistent efforts are much appreciated!

My wonderful brother Matt, thanks for always encouraging me to be engaged on a project. You are a great example of tenacity, and I appreciate your role in teaching me to finish a job.

To all of my friends and colleagues, and to everyone who liked, shared, and recommended this book to others, thank you for supporting this series. Community, friendship, and safe relationships are essential to providing the environment where growth can take place.

To all of the young people who have read this book, had the courage to evaluate self, established goals, and implemented habits, you will make a difference in your circle of influence. Never discount the impact you have simply by being your best you!

BIBLIOGRAPHY

Duhigg, Charles. *The Power of Habit: Why We Do What We Do in Life and Business* Random House, 2012.

"Metacognition." *Merriam-Webster Online Dictionary*, 2018, https://www.merriam-webster.com. Accessed 14 March, 2018.